W9-AGW-745

This Starfish Bay book belongs to

....

ELENA'S SHELLS

By Rose Robbins

FOR MERLIN

Elena loved collecting shells.

One day, right in the middle of her lunch, a very surprising thing happened.

One of her shells ran away!

Elena chased it over the sand dunes...

under the palm trees...

around the rocks...

and right to the ocean!

Before the shell could reach the ocean,
Elena had a bright idea.

SHARK!

The shell screeched to a halt.

"Why did you run away?
You naughty thing!"

Elena scolded, shaking the
shell up and down until...

PLOP!

A tiny creature fell out.

"Who are you?" asked Elena.

"I am a hermit crab!" explained the creature.

"I chose this shell when my old one got too small."

"It is my home!"

"Well, I found it first, so it's MINE."
Elena turned her back on the shell-less crab.

...But back home, something didn't feel right.

Elena worried about the little crab, all alone and with no shell to hide in. What would happen to him?

"I have enough shells of my own. I can spare just one."
Elena decided to go back and find the crab.

But was she too late?

"Get back, or I'll pinch you!" The crab was safe!

"I'm sorry I took your shell. Please take it back. You need it more than me." Elena offered the shell to the crab.

"Thank you!" squeaked the crab, cosy and safe once more.

Elena still loves to collect shells, but now she has friends to share her treasures with, and that is a lot more fun.

THE END.

Starfish Bay® Children's Books
An imprint of Starfish Bay Publishing
www.starfishbaypublishing.com

ELENA'S SHELLS

© Rose Robbins, 2019
ISBN 978-1-76036-057-3
First Published 2019
Printed in China by Beijing Shangtang Print & Packaging Co., Ltd.
11 Tengren Road, Niulanshan Town, Shunyi District, Beijing, China

This book is copyright. Apart from any fair dealing for the purpose of private study, research, criticism or review, as permitted under the Copyright Act, no part of this publication may be reproduced or transmitted in any form or by any means without the prior written permission of the publisher.

Sincere thanks to Elyse Williams from Starfish Bay Children's Books for her creative efforts in preparing this edition for publication.

Rose Robbins is a children's book author and illustrator currently residing in Nottingham, United Kingdom. She has been making books since the age of 7 when she received a stapler for her birthday. As well as books, Rose makes ceramics, puppets, felt and soft toys. She can be found either stuck in a story, or thinking about a new story - anything to get out of doing the dishes or putting out the laundry.